This Walker book belongs to:

_____

For
Liz Wood and David Lloyd

First published 2012 by Walker Books Ltd
87 Vauxhall Walk, London SE11 5HJ

This edition published 2013

2 4 6 8 10 9 7 5 3 1

© 2012 Polly Dunbar

The right of Polly Dunbar to be identified as author/illustrator of this work
has been asserted by her in accordance with the Copyright, Designs and Patents Act 1988

This book has been typeset in Historical Fell Type Printed in China

British Library Cataloguing in Publication Data:
a catalogue record for this book is available from the British Library

ISBN 978-1-4063-4462-2

www.walker.co.uk

Arthur's
DREAM BOAT

Polly Dunbar

WALKER BOOKS
AND SUBSIDIARIES
LONDON · BOSTON · SYDNEY · AUCKLAND

One night Arthur
had a dream.

It was amazing.

"Wow!" said Arthur to his dog.

"Last night I had a dream."

"It was amazing,"
Arthur said to his brother.
"Last night I dreamt about
a pink and green boat
with a stripy mast."

TIPPETY
TAP TIPPETY
TAP

"Mum," Arthur called. "Last night I dreamt about a boat. It was pink and green with a stripy mast and lovely spotty sails."

"Hey!" shouted Arthur to his sister. "Last night I dreamt about a boat. It was pink and green with a stripy mast and spotty sails, and it had a golden flag."

SPLITTER
SPLATTER
SPLODGE

"Dad!" cried Arthur.

"Last night I had a dream.

It was about a pink and green

boat with a stripy mast,

lovely spotty sails,

a golden flag and

a beautiful figurehead.

LISTEN TO ME!

I'm trying to tell you

about my ...

SSSHHH SSSHHH

"Ahoy!"

"Arthur!"

One night Arthur

had a dream.

And it really was ...

amazing!

POLLY DUNBAR

is a major star in the picture-book firmament.

She is the author/illustrator of *Penguin, Dog Blue* and *Flyaway Katie*,

and the illustrator of *Shoe Baby*, written by her mother, Joyce Dunbar.

The bestselling *Penguin* has won numerous national awards

and was shortlisted for the Kate Greenaway Medal.

Polly's six titles featuring Tilly, Hector, Tiptoe, Doodle,

Pru and Tumpty have been made into an animated TV series,

Tilly and Friends, shown on CBeebies.

Polly lives in Brighton.

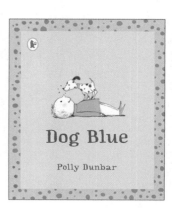

ISBN 978-1-84428-517-4   ISBN 978-1-4063-0161-8   ISBN 978-1-4063-1246-1   ISBN 978-1-84428-514-3

Available from all good booksellers

www.walker.co.uk